FRANKENFROG

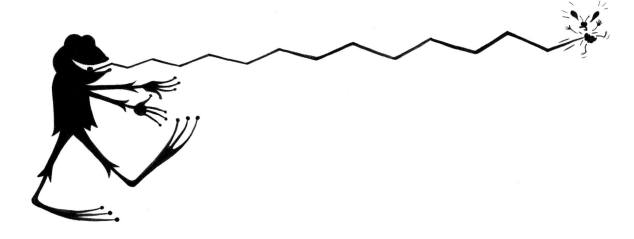

KIM KENNEDY

Illustrated by

DOUG KENNEDY

HYPERION BOOKS FOR CHILDREN
NEW YORK

FIRST EDITION

1 3 5 7 9 10 8 6 4 2

Printed in Hong Kong by South China Printing Company Ltd.

Library of Congress Cataloging-in-Publication Data
Kennedy, Kim.
Frankenfrog/Kim Kennedy; illustrated by Doug Kennedy.—1st ed.
p. cm.
Summary: After accidentally creating a monster fly, a mad scientist is obliged
to create an enormous frog to eliminate the pest.
ISBN 0-7868-0373-8 (trade)—ISBN 0-7868-2323-2 (library)
[1. Flies—Fiction. 2. Frogs—Fiction.] I. Kennedy, Doug, ill. II. Title.
PZ7.K3843Fr 1999
[E]—dc21 98–44740

To all the frogs
that never made it out
of the seventh-grade
biology lab.

Dr. Franken, the mad scientist, was famous for his many strange inventions.

He developed
the world's first
BOTTLED LAUGH,

the **CLOSET-MONSTER**

detector,

and the incredible
HYPER-SIZING

tonic, which worked

wonders on lollipops!

It just so happened that while Dr. Franken and his helpers, the Mungers, were chomping on some giant candy, a fly took a nosedive into the hyper-sizing tonic and emerged as . . .

Geronimooooooooo

. . . a hideous **HYPERFLY—**
a droolish, ghoulish creature that
towered over the doctor and his
Mungers!

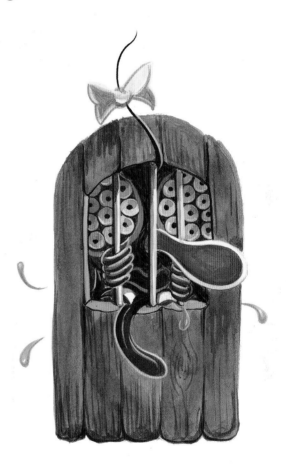

With much trouble, they trapped the
buzzing beast in the cellar, where it was
forgotten.

But not for long.

Soon Dr. Franken was
preparing another experiment.
But just when it was ready to conduct,
tiny, pesky flies began appearing, sticking
to wires and buzzing into tubes.
"WHERE IN THE SCIENTIFIC WORLD
ARE THESE FLIES COMING FROM?" Dr. Franken demanded.
Just then, a bone-chilling **BZZZZZzzzz** came from the cellar.
"Of course!" he cried. "The Hyperfly! It's MULTIFLYING!"
How could he rid the lab of all those flies?

chicken   to a swan

An idea struck him. "Only a frog could get rid of so many flies! But not *any* old frog. An electrical specimen that only a mastermind such as I can create!"

"Go to Croaking Acres," he instructed the Mungers, "and bring me back a frightfully large frog. *Hurry!*"

They fetched
the biggest one
they could find.

Dr. Franken got to work on the amphibian,
hooking it to leap-electrodes, croak-conductors,
and tongue-transformers. Finally, Dr. Franken cried,
"Throw the switch!"

Sparks flew! Wires crackled! The lab hummed with energy!

The frog's legs gave a twitch and a hop.

Then from its wide green mouth came a long, slow

"Ribbbittt."

"IT'S ALIVE!" cried Dr. Franken. "BEHOLD . . .

FRANKENFROG!"

"**Ribbbittt,**" he croaked,

hopping from the table with a watery *SPLAT*.

"Me . . . want . . . SWAMP!"

"Never mind the swamp," said the doctor. "Devour those flies!"

Frankenfrog fired his tongue at the insects, blitzing them with an air-splitting **ZAP!**

"Excellent work!" praised the doctor, patting his creation on its slimy, luminous head.

"Now for the Hyperfly!" said Dr. Franken, unlocking the cellar door. "Get rid of that freaky fly factory!"

"Me go to swamp!" bellowed Frankenfrog.

"Mungers!" Dr. Franken shouted. "Stop him! Stop him!"

But the Mungers were no match for the stinging, ringing **ZAP!** of Frankenfrog's tongue. He zapped the doctor's tornado tunnel and misty molecular pool. He zapped the atomic-fusion funnel and tubes of electro-plasm drool.

"Me go to swamp!" he croaked. And in a blur of tongue and webbed feet, Frankenfrog was gone, vanished into the foggy night.

Down in the swamp an amphibious affair was being held, every lily pad piled to the tip-top with frolicking boghoppers. From the shadows, Frankenfrog watched his fellow-kind. How he longed to leap with them! But now he was a freakish frog, a glowing goofball, a megavolt mess.

As the jitterbugs jittered and the wood ducks twittered, his urge to join them grew stronger and stronger.

With a collosal **"CROAK!"** Frankenfrog
jumped into their midst, sending shock waves
through the swamp.

"An electrified frog!" quacked a frantic duck.
"Everyone out of the water!" The swamp was swept
into a panic. There had never been so much flapping,
flopping, swimming, and hopping!

"Come back!" called Frankenfrog. But it was no use.
All alone, Frankenfrog slumped on a stump, his glow
growing dimmer. What would he do now? he wondered.
Would the doctor take him back, after making such a
mess? "Probably n-o-t," sighed Frankenfrog. "I'll just fade
away into the dark."

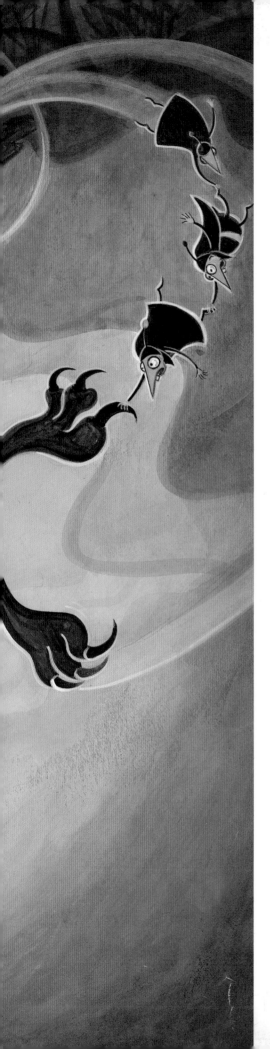

Suddenly, he heard a bone-chilling
BZZZZZzzz followed by a pitiful "HELP!"
Frankenfrog turned to see the Hyperfly
buzzing over the swamp, with Dr. Franken in
its grasp.

Taking aim, Frankenfrog fired away, but
the Hyperfly, with its supersonic wings,
dodged the *ZAPS* and ducked the *ZINGS*.

"Hurry!" begged Dr. Franken. But try as he
might, Frankenfrog couldn't muster one more
zap. He was all tapped out! I need an electric
charge, he thought. But where would he get
one?

Licking her lips, the hungry Hyperfly leered.

Oh, what *would* she feast on first? A Dr. Franken filet?

Or some crunchy Munger munchies? She opened her slobbering

snout for a mouthful of . . .

With an electrifying leap, Frankenfrog met the monstrous fly with a supercharged jolt right between her eyes. Her antennae corkscrewed, her wings crisscrossed, and with a stupendous **POW!** she disintegrated into a crackling cloud of flydust!

"You saved us!" cheered the doctor. Then, from the shadows crept the swamp critters.

"Wow!" they cheered. "What an electrical spectacle!"

"For the sake of science," said the puzzled doctor, "where did you get the energy to blow up that nasty mutant?"

Frankenfrog croaked, and out of his mouth flew a giant cloud of fireflies.

"Edible electricity!" cried Dr. Franken. *"How ingenious!"*

So the doctor, his Mungers, and Frankenfrog returned to the castle, to the world of bubbles, potions, and magnificent notions.

And they lived *zappily* ever after. That is, until Dr. Franken's next experiment . . .